Mr Trim and Miss Jumble

Written and illustrated by

Ed Boxall

WALKER BOOKS
AND SUBSIDIARIES
LONDON · BOSTON · SYDNEY · AUCKLAND

Chapter One

Mr Trim was a teacher.
This is how he looked:

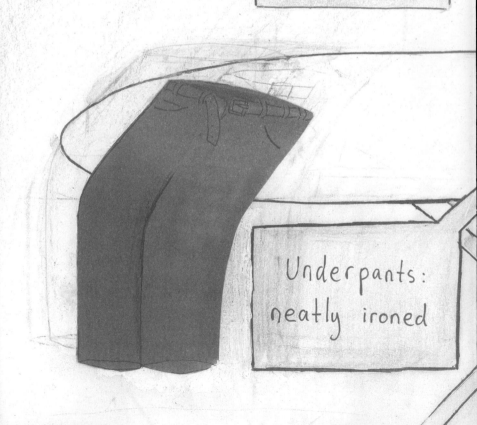

Shirt:
neatly
pressed

Underpants:
neatly ironed

The children in Mr Trim's class were just like Mr Trim.

Their hair was always neat...

Their uniforms were always neat...

Their work was always neat...

Their handwriting always sat politely on the line.

And they always tucked their chairs neatly under their tables.

The children always tried to
behave well. If they didn't,
Mr Trim made them stay behind
and tidy up. They had to iron
every page of his newspaper ...

sweep the playground with
a paintbrush ...

When everyone else had gone home, Mr Trim would tidy Quentin, the class hamster. He was very fond of Quentin – in fact, Quentin was Mr Trim's only friend.

Chapter Two

One day Mr Trim woke up feeling ill. It was nothing serious – just a bubbly nose and a fuzzy head – but his doctor ordered him to stay in bed.

Mon	Tues	Weds	Thurs	Fri	Sat	Sun
1 ←moan→	2	3	4 go to doctor's	5 ←groan	6 →	7
8 ←whinge→	9	10	11 feel better	12 ←snivel	13 →	14
15	16	17	18	19	20	21
22	23	24	25	26	27	28
29	30					

A supply teacher came
to look after his class.

The supply teacher was called Miss Jumble. This is how she looked:

Miss Jumble was not tidy at all.
In fact, she left a trail of
untidiness wherever she went.
On Monday she un-tidied the
classroom.

On Tuesday she un-tidied
the cookery room.

On Wednesday she un-tidied
the music teacher.

On Thursday she un-tidied the art room.

And on Friday there was a school trip to the museum. Miss Jumble un-tidied the museum as well!

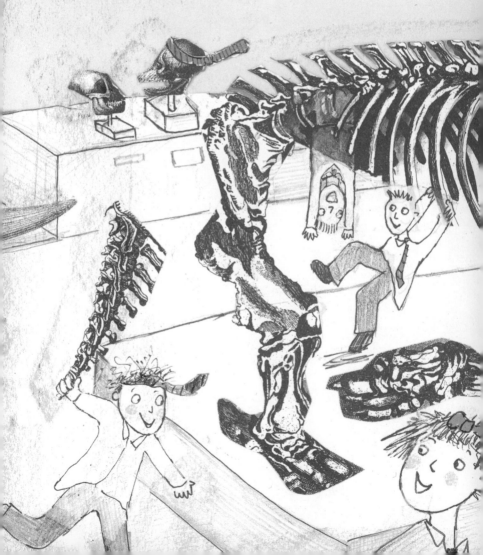

After a week with Miss Jumble the children looked like this:

Chapter Three

Miss Jumble was monstrously messy, but she was also fantastic fun. In Maths she took the class bowling. She covered up the screen so you had to add up your own score.

Strike!

In Geography she took everyone mapreading in the woods.

In History everyone dressed up as knights and princesses.

And in Science, there was a
new sound in class – laughter!
The children loved Miss Jumble.
But now and again, they thought
it might be nice to have Mr Trim
back for a few hours...

Giggle

Giggle

Giggle

Just for a bit of peace and quiet.

Chapter Four

Mr Trim did come back.
When he saw what Miss Jumble
had done to the classroom
he looked like this:

And when he saw what Miss Jumble had done to the children he looked like this:

But when he saw that Quentin's cage door was open and THERE WAS NO SIGN OF QUENTIN ... he looked like this:

"Oh dear," said
Miss Jumble.
"We'll find
him ... don't
worry."

They looked under the tables...

They looked behind the cupboards...

They looked in the toilets...

But they couldn't find Quentin
anywhere.

"Er, miss," said Judy, "don't you think Jimbo is looking especially well fed today?"
Everyone looked at the school cat.

The nice children gasped.
The not-so-nice children
sniggered.
Mr Trim whimpered.

But just at that moment a tiny
black nose snuffled out of Miss
Jumble's hair. It was Quentin,
who had been having a snooze.

When he saw Mr Trim, he gave a happy squeak and leapt onto his shoulder.

All the nice children went "Ah".

All the not-so-nice children made being-sick noises.

And at that moment something
else happened. Mr Trim looked
deep into Miss Jumble's eyes.
Miss Jumble looked deep
into Mr Trim's eyes.

They blushed.
Their hearts fluttered.

All the nice children went "Ah" again. And all the not-so-nice children made being-sick noises again.

And everyone, including Quentin,

lived happily ever after.

For my family

First published 2005 by Walker Books Ltd
87 Vauxhall Walk, London SE11 5HJ

2 4 6 8 10 9 7 5 3 1

The right of Ed Boxall to be identified as
author of this work has been asserted by him in accordance
with the Copyright, Designs and Patents Act 1988

This book has been typeset in Frutiger Roman

Printed in China

British Library Cataloguing in Publication Data:
a catalogue record for this book is available
from the British Library

ISBN 1-84428-955-9

www.walkerbooks.co.uk